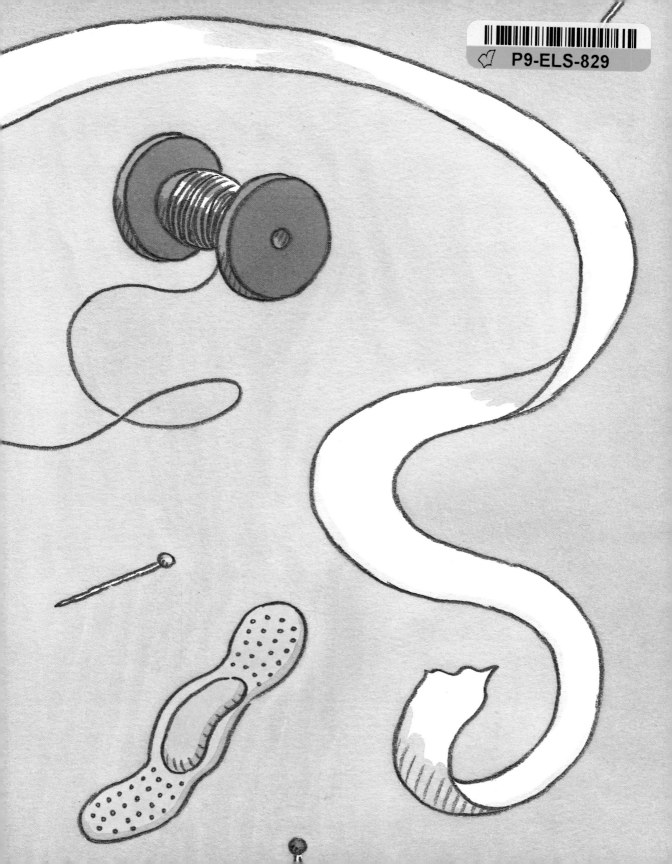

First U.S. edition
First published in Great Britain in 1992
by Walker Books Ltd., London

ISBN 1-56402-035-5

Library of Congress Catalog Card Number 91-71830
Library of Congress Cataloging-in-Publication information is available.

10 9 8 7 6 5 4 3 2 1

Printed and bound by L.E.G.O., Vicenza, Italy.

Candlewick Press
2067 Massachusetts Avenue
Cambridge, Massachusetts 02140

My Old Teddy

by Dom Mansell

CANDLEWICK PRESS
CAMBRIDGE, MASSACHUSETTS

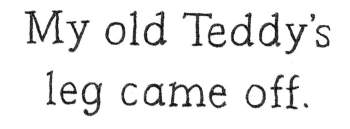

My old Teddy's
leg came off.

Poor old Teddy!

I took him to the Teddy doctor.

She made Teddy better.

My old Teddy's arm came off.

Poor old Teddy!

I took him to the
Teddy doctor.

She made Teddy better.

My old Teddy's ear came off.

Poor old Teddy!

I took him to the Teddy doctor.

She made Teddy better.

Then poor old Teddy's head came off.

The Teddy doctor
said, "Teddy's had
enough now."

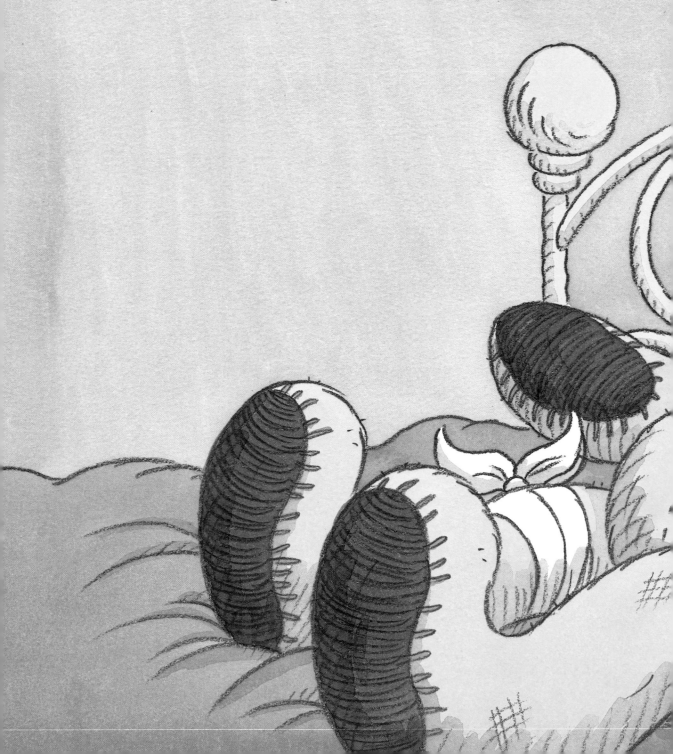

"Teddy has to rest."

The Teddy doctor gave me...

a new Teddy.

I love my new Teddy
very much,

but I love
poor old Teddy best.
Dear old,
poor
old
Teddy.

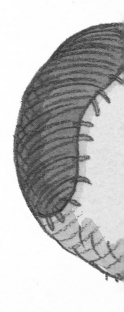

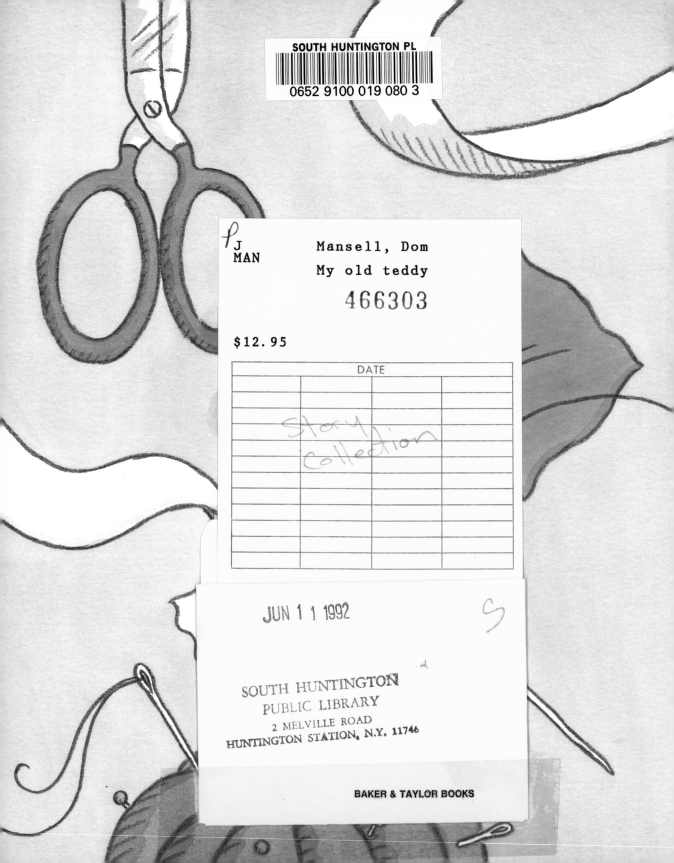